DATE DUE

GRUESOME GOBLIN

Written by
James Gelsey

A
LITTLE APPLE
PAPERBACK

SCHOLASTIC INC.

New York Toronto London Auckland Sydney
Mexico City New Delhi Hong Kong Buenos Aires

For Beth

ISBN 0-439-42076-8

Designed by Carisa Swenson

12 11 10 9 8 7 6 5 4 3   4 5 6 7 8 9/0

Special thanks to Duendes del Sur for cover and interior illustrations.
Printed in the U.S.A.
First printing, April 2004

Chapter 1

The sun was shining as Fred drove the Mystery Machine. down the highway. Everyone in the van was wearing sunglasses.

"Man, I thought the sun would, like, never come out again," Shaggy said.

"Even though I don't like to exaggerate, I have to agree with Shaggy," Velma said. "Those two straight weeks of rain were the worst."

"You said it, Velma," Daphne agreed. "Now we're finally able to use our season passes to Ocean Land."

"Speaking of Ocean Land," Fred said, "there it is." He pointed to a large, blue water tower in the distance. The tower stood amid a tangle of tubes, slides, and other water park rides.

"Hey, Scoob, we're almost there!" Shaggy called. "Let's get ready." Shaggy ducked into the back of the van.

"But they're already wearing bathing suits," Daphne said. "What do you think they have to do to get ready?"

"I'm afraid to find out," Velma answered.

Fred drove past a huge Ocean Land sign.

"Hey, isn't that Tippy Torrance's picture?" asked Daphne. "I didn't know she was associated with Ocean Land."

Shaggy and Scooby poked their heads up front. Each wore a mask and snorkel.

"Who's Trippy Torrance?" Shaggy asked.

Velma and Daphne turned and looked. Shaggy and Scooby were dressed in wet suits.

"I know I'm going to be sorry I asked this," Velma began, "but why are you two wearing wet suits?"

"For the Flume Plume," Shaggy said. "We don't want to get too wet, right, pal?"

"Rou ret!" Scooby barked.

"But we're going to a water park," Daphne said. "You're supposed to get wet."

"We know that, Daph," Shaggy said. "But this way we can keep our snacks dry when we go on the water rides. Show 'em, Scooby."

Scooby reached into his wet suit and

pulled out a mushed peanut butter, banana, and chocolate chip sandwich.

"Oh, brother," Velma moaned.

Scooby took a bite of his sandwich and put the rest back into his wet suit.

"Now who's Troppy Tippance?" asked Shaggy.

"Tippy Torrance," Fred said. "She's a swimmer who won four gold medals at the

Olympics last year. It looks like she's doing celebrity endorsements for Ocean Land."

"Cool," Shaggy said. "So while Scooby and I are on the Flume Plume, what are you all going to be doing?"

"Freddy and I are going to check out the Surfer's Lagoon," Daphne said.

"And I'm interested in the Wave Pool," Velma said. "I want to test one of my theories about the frequency and amplitude of certain wave formations."

As Fred drove into the parking lot, he noticed a long trail of cars heading out.

"That's strange," Velma said. "It's barely eleven in the morning, and look at all the people leaving."

Fred found a spot near the front gate and parked the van. As the gang got out, Daphne walked over to a woman who was leaving with her three children.

"Excuse me," Daphne said. "But my friends

and I just got here. Is everything all right? Is the park closed?"

"I don't know if it is, but it sure should be," the woman answered angrily. "The Whirlpool adventure ride got so rough that my kids were tossed from their inner tubes. And the waves at the Wave Pool were so high, they kept knocking everybody over. This place is not safe!"

"They'll probably shut down those two

rides and keep the rest of the park open," Velma said.

"As long as the Flume Plume is still fluming and pluming, nothing will keep Scooby and me away from Ocean Land," Shaggy announced.

Just then, a loud scream pierced the air.

"Zoinks!" Shaggy cried, jumping into Scooby's arms. "Except that!"

Chapter 2

The gang showed their season passes and ran through the entry gate. There they saw a little kid crying his eyes out. He stood in front of a snow cone stand with a pile of greenish ice in his hand. His mother stood next to him.

"I demand to see the park manager!" she shouted. "Where is the manager? I'm going to call my lawyer!"

A woman in a blue-and-yellow Ocean Land shirt ran over. After a few moments of conversation, the boy stopped crying and the mother smiled. As the mother and son walked back into the park, the woman in the Ocean Land shirt examined the snow cone stand.

"Hey, that's Tippy Torrance!" Daphne said. "I wonder how she was able to get that boy to stop crying."

"One way to find out," Velma said. She walked over to the snow cone stand. "Excuse me, Ms. Torrance."

Tippy Torrance spun around and smiled at Velma. "Oh, call me Tippy. How can I help you?" she asked in a friendly Southern accent.

"My friends and I were wondering how you managed to get that boy to smile," Velma said. "He seemed pretty upset."

"He sure was." Tippy nodded. "He said that some weird-looking creature in an Ocean Land uniform served

9

up the snow cone in his hand. Then the creature laughed and ran away. I told him that was how we picked the winners of the Ocean Land season pass contest."

"I didn't know there was a season pass contest," Fred said.

"There is now," Tippy said. "I had to come up with something to keep those folks happy and in the park. We've had a lot of mysterious goings-on lately, and they're beginning to affect attendance."

"Then maybe it's time for you to bail out of Ocean Land," a man said from behind Tippy. "No sense having your good name tarnished by a bad water park."

"Well, if it isn't Bruno Meisterhoffen," Tippy said. "Listen, Bruno, I bought Ocean Land to make it one of the best family water parks in the world. I'm not going to let anyone or anything scare me away."

Bruno's red-white-and-blue shirt scrunched up as he shrugged his shoulders. "Suit yourself, Tippy," he said with a laugh. "Get it? *Suit* your-self? As in swimsuit? 'Cause you're a famous swimmer?"

Shaggy and Scooby giggled. Tippy, Fred, Daphne, and Velma just stood in silence.

"At least hear me out, Tippy," Bruno said, becoming serious again. "I've just purchased that old industrial park down the road. I'll have the Bruno Meisterhoffen Water Polo Stadium built there by next summer. Think of it, Tippy. With your star power and my money, we can host the international water polo championships."

Bruno fumbled in his pockets for something. He took out a piece of paper and unfolded it. "Take a look at this," he said proudly.

Tippy looked at the picture. Her eyes widened in horror.

"Hey, like, that's you!" Shaggy said, pointing at Tippy.

"Wearing the official red-white-and-blue water polo uniform of the Meisterhoffen Plumbing Supply water polo team," Bruno said proudly.

"But I've never worn a swimsuit like that before," Tippy said. "Where did you get that picture?"

"I took that photo of you from the Ocean Land brochure and scanned it into my computer," Bruno said. "Then it was just a matter of a few mouse clicks to create this."

Fred, Daphne, and Velma could see the anger rising in Tippy's face. She was starting to turn red.

"Excuse me, Bruno," she said through clenched teeth. "But I have work to do. Good-bye."

With that, she turned and walked away, focusing her attention on a family that was walking toward the exit.

"She'll come around," Bruno said with a smile. "She'll come around." He walked away and disappeared into the crowd.

"I wonder what kind of weird creature would dress up like a snow cone salesman," Daphne asked.

"Like, take a look and find out!" Shaggy grinned.

Fred, Daphne, and Velma turned and saw

Scooby-Doo standing behind the snow cone stand. He wore a pointed snow cone hat over his wet suit.

"Ro rone, ranyone?" he asked.

"Very funny, Scooby," Velma said. "But this is no time for joking around."

"I'll say," Shaggy agreed. "It's time for some water fun! Last one to the Flume Plume is a soggy Scooby Snack!"

Chapter 3

Shaggy and Scooby ran toward the Flume Plume. As they passed the Water Playground, a guy on a skateboard zipped out of nowhere. Shaggy and Scooby ducked as the skateboarder and his board flew into the air. They watched as the guy finally landed, and roared to a stop, sending sparks flying.

"Awesome!" he gasped.

Shaggy and Scooby stood up slowly, nervously.

"Sorry about that," the skateboarder said as he walked over to Shaggy and Scooby. "Totally my fault, dude and dude-dog. I so wasn't looking where I was going. Are you all right?"

"We're fine," Shaggy said. "But I don't think you're going to be. Look." The skateboarder turned and saw Tippy Torrance running over.

"Busted," he moaned.

"Ziggy Bones, how many times have I told you not to ride your skateboard in the park?" Tippy asked.

"I can't help it," Ziggy replied. "My board has a mind of its own."

"I told you the last time that if I caught you riding that thing in here I was going to confiscate it," Tippy said. "Now hand it over."

"Harsh, dudette, very harsh," Ziggy said.

"What's going on?" asked Daphne. "Did Shaggy and Scooby get into trouble, Tippy?"

Tippy shook her head and glared at Ziggy Bones.

"Guilty," Ziggy said, raising his hand.

"Ziggy here thinks that Ocean Land is his personal skateboard park," Tippy said, "even though he knows how dangerous that is."

"But that's only because there are all these people around playing in the water," Ziggy said. "Take away the water and this place would make a supreme-o skateboarder's par-

adise. Just look around, Tippy. The Flume Plume, the Whirlpool, even the Lazy River is like the ultimate half-pipe. Take it from the Zigster. This place could become the center of the skateboarding universe."

Before Tippy could answer, Fred noticed something on the ground next to Ziggy's skateboard. He picked up a piece of paper. "What's this?" he wondered.

Ziggy saw it and his eyes widened.

"Uh, that's my, uh, skateboarding license," Ziggy fumbled. "I'll just take that." But before he could get it, Tippy snatched it from Fred. She unfolded the paper, then rolled her eyes.

"It's just a concept, Tippy," Ziggy said. "Really, just something I was messing with on the computer."

She showed the gang the piece of paper.

"Hey, it's another picture of you, Tippy," Daphne said.

"Only in this one I'm on a skateboard in-

stead of wearing a water polo uniform," Tippy said.

"Like I said, it was just an idea," Ziggy said, taking the paper from Tippy and stuffing it into his pocket.

Tippy took a deep breath and smiled at Ziggy. "I know you mean well, Ziggy," she said. "But I'm a swimmer, not a skateboarder. You can pick up your skateboard at the security office later."

"The Zigster is saddened to hear that,"

Ziggy said. "Maybe you'll change your mind one day. And when you do, I'll be ready." Ziggy trudged off into the park.

"Golly, Tippy," Daphne said. "It seems like everyone wants you to do something for them."

"I know," Tippy said. "Ever since I won those gold medals, people only see me as a way to make money for them. They don't realize I'm not into that sort of thing."

Tippy's walkie-talkie squawked, telling her she was needed at the Flume Plume.

"I've gotta run," Tippy said. "Catch up with you later." Tippy ran off. She was still carrying Ziggy's skateboard.

"The Flume Plume?" Shaggy said. "Like, that's where Scooby and I want to go."

"I hope everything's all right over there," Velma said.

"Let's go find out," Fred said.

Chapter 4

*B*efore Shaggy and Scooby could start toward the Flume Plume, Fred, Daphne, and Velma stood right in front of them, blocking their path.

"Oh, no you don't," Velma said.

"We're not taking another step until you two get out of those ridiculous outfits," Daphne said.

"But if we take off our wet suits, all our snacks will get, like, wet," Shaggy said.

"Shaggy, you're not allowed to take food on the rides," Velma pointed out.

"Okay, you guys win," Shaggy said.

"Come on, Scoob. Let's use that cabana over there."

Shaggy and Scooby walked over to a large wooden shed. They opened the door and stepped inside.

"Hey!" a voice yelled from inside the shed.

Shaggy and Scooby backed out of the shed. An old man wearing coveralls and carrying a toolbox followed them.

"Like, sorry," Shaggy said. "We didn't realize this cabana was taken."

"Cabana, my eye," the old man said. "This is the pump house for Ocean Land attraction number eight: the Whirlpool. Authorized personnel only."

Daphne glanced at the man's Ocean Land name tag. "Sorry, Mr. Glumley," she said. "Our friends were just looking for someplace to change."

"How about trying the locker rooms at Happy Sally Land across town?" the man snapped. "That's where I'm headed."

"But don't you work here?" Velma asked.

"Not since about an hour ago, when Tippy Torrance fired me," Mr. Glumley said. "Blamed me for the crazy goings-on at the Whirlpool. I told her I didn't do it, but she said that since I was head of maintenance, I had to take responsibility for it."

Mr. Glumley shook his head sadly and looked down at his toolbox. "I've been working at Ocean Land ever since it opened," he said. "I helped build some of these water rides. And now someone's going around messing with the water pressure, and I get fired."

"Maybe if you speak to Tippy —" Velma began.

"She doesn't care about anything but her reputation," Mr. Glumley interrupted. "She wants to fire me, fine. She'll get hers one day."

As Mr. Glumley turned to leave, a piece of

paper flew out of his toolbox. Scooby picked it up and giggled. He showed it to Shaggy, who also giggled. It was a picture of Tippy Torrance with some of her teeth blacked out and a mustache drawn on.

Daphne looked at it and took it away from Scooby. "Uh, Mr. Glumley, I think you dropped something," she called.

Mr. Glumley saw the paper in her hand and blushed. He ran over and grabbed it

away. "All right, so I got a little carried away," he said. "It's a free country." He stuffed the paper into his coveralls and walked away.

"Jeepers, I've never seen anyone so angry before," Daphne said.

"I say let's forget about Mr. Glumley and go see what's happening at the Flume Plume," Fred said.

"Great idea, Fredd-o," Shaggy said.

"Right after you two change out of those wet suits," Daphne added.

After Shaggy and Scooby changed, the gang walked through Ocean Land to the Flume Plume, the tallest ride in the park. They saw Tippy standing at the entrance.

"Is everything okay here, Ms. Torrance?" asked Fred.

"Seems to be," Tippy answered. "A couple of kids say they saw something strange running behind the ride. But I checked it out and couldn't find anything. Probably just a prank."

"So does that mean the Flume Plume is open?" Shaggy asked eagerly.

"Prepare yourself for the wettest, wildest ride in the world!" Tippy said. She stepped aside and motioned Shaggy and Scooby toward the ride. "This is usually the longest line in the park. But so many people have left, you won't have to wait at all."

"We'll meet you at the Surfer's Lagoon!" Daphne called.

Halfway toward the ride, Shaggy stopped.
"Hey, Daphne!" he called. "Catch!"

He tossed something into the air that landed with a splat at Daphne's feet.

"What is it?" asked Fred.

Daphne looked down at her peanut butter-and-banana-splattered feet.

"Shaggy's and Scooby's lunch!" she moaned.

Chapter 5

The winding path to the top of the Flume Plume took Shaggy and Scooby through a fake forest. Enormous redwood trees towered over them. The chirps and squawks of forest critters filled the air. Shaggy and Scooby couldn't even hear the sounds of Ocean Land anymore.

"Man, I don't know about you, Scooby, but this is just a little too creepy for me," Shaggy said.

"Reah, reepy," Scooby agreed. "Rhere ris reverybody?"

"Probably hanging ten with Fred and Daphne at the Surfer's Lagoon," Shaggy said.

As they neared the top of the forest path, a roaring sound filled their ears. It was the giant waterfall at the top of the Flume Plume. Shaggy and Scooby walked into a small wooden pavilion. An Ocean Land employee wearing a blue poncho pointed to the giant log bobbing up and down in front of them. The worker guided them into the log. He locked down the lap bar and stepped back into the pavilion.

"Have fun!" he yelled. "And if you're scared of heights, don't look down!"

"Don't what?" Shaggy shouted back.

"Look down!" the employee shouted back.

Scooby and Shaggy both looked down and realized how high they were.

"Rikes!" Scooby yelled, covering his eyes.

"Zoinks!" Shaggy cried, doing the same.

Shaggy and Scooby felt the log lurch for-

ward. The rushing water pushed the log
along the giant flume, curving this way and
that. Just as the log reached the edge of the giant drop, it stopped.

Scooby took his paws away from his eyes.
"Ruh?" he said. "Rhat rhappened?"

"Like, I don't know, Scoob," Shaggy said. He looked over the side and saw that all of the water had stopped. The log teetered on the edge. "Don't move, Scooby, or we'll end up fluming without the pluming."

"Attention, Ocean Land!"

Shaggy and Scooby looked up and saw a blue creature standing on top of the Ocean

Land water tower just behind the Flume Plume pavilion. From what they could see, the creature had large, pointy ears and a mean-looking face.

"I am King of the Goblins!" the creature announced as it held up a long metal scepter of some kind. "Ocean Land is officially closed!" The creature's amplified voice echoed throughout the park.

"Man, I've got a 'zoinks' inside of me that's dying to get out," Shaggy said through clenched teeth.

"Ron't roo rit," Scooby said.

"I'm trying, pal, I'm trying," Shaggy said.

"Leave now, and no one will get hurt," the goblin continued. "And if you don't, I will turn Ocean Land into Goblin Land!"

With a sinister cackle, the goblin disappeared down the side of the tower. A moment later, the waterfall behind the Flume Plume roared back to life. Shaggy and Scooby felt their log start bobbing in the water again.

"Hold on, Scooby!" Shaggy yelled.

The swell of water from the waterfall pushed the log over the edge.

"HEEEEEEEELLLLLLLLLLLLLPPPPPPPPPP!" Shaggy and Scooby screamed as they hurtled

down the flume. They splashed along, sending an enormous tidal wave into the sky.

Fred, Daphne, Velma, and Tippy came running over. Tippy helped them out of the log.

"Are you two all right?" she asked.

Dripping wet, Shaggy and Scooby looked at each other and smiled.

"Awesome!" they declared in unison.

"Well, I'm glad you're all right," Tippy said. "But now someone has shut off the water at the Lazy River. Things are falling apart all over the place."

A throng of park visitors ran by Tippy and the gang, heading directly for the exit.

"Once word about this goblin thing gets out, I'll be ruined," Tippy said. "Ocean Land will have to close."

"Not if we have anything to say about it," Fred said. "Ms. Torrance, you go take care of the crowd. Leave the gruesome goblin to us!"

Chapter 6

"Okay, gang, we've got to act fast if we want to help keep Ocean Land open," Fred said. "I say we split up and look for clues."

"I say we split up and have snow cones," Shaggy said.

"When we came over before, Ms. Torrance said that two kids saw a strange creature run behind the ride," Velma recalled. "I have a hunch they saw the goblin on its way to the water tower."

"Good point, Velma," Fred said. "Take Shaggy and Scooby with you. Daphne and I will start with the Whirlpool, where the trouble first happened today."

"Let's meet back at the Lazy River by the front gate," Daphne said. "Whoever gets there first can look around for clues."

Behind the Flume Plume entrance, Velma found a gate with a NO ADMITTANCE sign on it. She opened the gate and peered inside. "This is the way," she said. "Come on."

Velma led Shaggy and Scooby down a path to the water tower. At the base of the enormous structure, Shaggy and Scooby noticed a ladder that reached up the side of the tower, all the way to the top. They looked up and froze.

"Don't be such scaredy-cats," Velma said. "It's all mind over matter. Just pretend you're climbing a ladder to change a lightbulb."

"Man, the only lightbulb you'd change by climbing this ladder is the one inside the sun," Shaggy said. "How about Scooby and I look for clues on the ground first?"

"Rike ris," Scooby said. He put his nose to

the ground and began sniffing around. As he sniffed, a piece of paper got sucked up against his nose.

"Good job, Scooby," Velma said as she examined the torn piece of paper. "It looks like part of a picture of someone. But why would the goblin have something like this?"

"You know, Velma, that really doesn't matter," Shaggy said. "What matters is that now Scooby and I can get a snow cone."

"Right!" Scooby agreed.

Velma peered over her glasses at Shaggy. "Maybe later, fellas," she said. "Let's take this clue over to the Lazy River. We'll look around there while we're waiting for Fred and Daphne."

The three of them walked back into the water park.

"Jinkies, this place has really emptied out," Velma said. "I don't think there's anyone else here but us."

"And one gruesome, bluesome goblin," Shaggy said.

They found the Lazy River and looked inside. Blue and red inner tubes lay scattered along the empty river's cement bottom.

"Rhere's rhe river?" Scooby asked.

"I don't know, Scoob," Shaggy said. "But I do know that those inner tubes are making me hungry."

"How can inner tubes make you hungry?" asked Velma.

"Because they look like giant red and blue doughnuts," Shaggy said.

"Roughnuts," Scooby echoed. "Rummy!"

"Shaggy, please try to keep your mind on the clues," Velma said. "Now I'm going to look around over there. You and Scooby see if you can find any doughnuts — I mean, clues — over here."

Shaggy and Scooby walked to the empty river's edge and looked down.

"Nothing down here but an assortment of

glazed, powdered, and chocolate-covered inner tubes," Shaggy reported with a giggle. "Hey, what's that?"

Shaggy jumped into the empty riverbed and picked up a pair of sunglasses. "Someone left in such a hurry they forgot their sunglasses, Scooby," Shaggy said. "Look, there's another pair over there."

Scooby followed him and put on the other pair. As Shaggy and Scooby admired each other, they felt their feet get wet.

"Hey, what's going on?" Shaggy asked. He looked down and saw a trickle of water build into a flowing stream. Soon the stream became a rapid current of water.

"The river's filling up!" Shaggy cried. "It's the goblin! It's trying to drown us!"

Chapter 7

Shaggy and Scooby tried to climb up the sides of the river, but the cement was too slippery from the water. They grabbed onto some inner tubes and floated around the river.

"Help! The goblin's trying to drown us!" Shaggy called.

"Relax, you two," Velma called from the side of the river. "It's just me. I found the pump house for the Lazy River. I also found this and used it to turn on the water." She held up a long metal wrench.

"Hey, isn't that the goblin king's royal scepter?" Shaggy asked.

"It's also a clue," Velma said. "I'm going to find Fred and Daphne. Stay out of trouble."

"What kind of trouble can we get into?" asked Shaggy.

"Knowing the two of you, it could be anything!" Velma answered.

Shaggy and Scooby climbed out of the Lazy River.

"There's nothing like a lazy river ride to build up an appetite, right, Scooby?" Shaggy said.

"Right!" Scooby barked.

Shaggy spied the snow cone stand right by the front gate.

"Hey, how about a snow cone?" asked Shaggy.

"Rokay," Scooby said.

They walked over to the stand.

"Hello? We'd like two snow cones, please," Shaggy said. "Hello? Is anyone here?"

As Shaggy and Scooby looked behind the snow cone counter, the goblin jumped up wearing a concession hat.

"Did someone ask for a snow cone?" it cackled. The goblin dumped a scoop of flavored ice onto Shaggy's head. Scooby started laughing. Then the goblin dumped a scoop of ice onto Scooby's head.

"Hey!" Shaggy said. "No one dumps snow cones on my pal!"

The goblin's smile turned into an angry scowl. "What are you going to do about it?" it demanded in a mean voice.

"Uh . . . run?" Shaggy said. "Let's go, Scooby!"

Shaggy and Scooby ran through the park with the goblin chasing after them. As they ran, the ice flew off their heads and pelted the goblin.

"Come back here!" the goblin shouted.

Shaggy and Scooby ran into the entrance to the Whirlpool and jumped into the over-size inner tubes. The tubes floated along a narrow chute and then fell into a giant pool. Enormous swirls of water caught the tubes and spun them around and around. Shaggy and Scooby heard the goblin's evil laugh and felt the water get rougher.

"Hold on, Scooby," Shaggy hollered over the roar of the water.

The tubes spun faster and faster as Shaggy and Scooby bounced around the Whirlpool. Then, just as quickly as it started, the water stopped churning and slowly drained out of the pool. Shaggy and Scooby walked to the exit, still clutching their inner tubes.

"Are you two okay?" asked Daphne. She and Fred stood next to the exit.

"Man, now I know what my socks feel like in the washing machine," Shaggy moaned. "Where is the goblin?"

"After it turned the ride up full blast, it ran away," Fred said. "It must have seen us coming."

"Velma used the tool she found to shut down the ride," Daphne said.

Shaggy and Scooby stepped out of their inner tubes. They were soaked from head to toe.

"I think I've had enough water fun for one day," Shaggy said. "What do you say we go back to the van and get our clothes?"

"Not quite yet, Shaggy," Fred said. "We've got one more thing to take care of first."

"What's that?" asked Shaggy. "Or don't I want to know?"

"Putting together the clues you and Velma found with what Daphne and I found," Fred said.

Daphne held out a curved piece of red-white-and-blue rubber.

"That's a nice bendy flag you've got there,

Daphne," Shaggy said. "Now where's the clue you and Fred found?"

"Shaggy, this is it," Daphne said. She draped the rubbery flag over her fist.

"Fits you like a glove," Shaggy joked.

"Or a hat," Daphne added with a knowing smile.

"And with this last clue, one thing has become crystal clear," Velma said. "Our goblin is all washed up."

"You know what that means, gang," Fred said. "It's time to set a trap!"

Chapter 8

"I've got a plan to capture the goblin by doing to it what it's already done to Shaggy and Scooby," Fred said.

"You mean you're going to dump a snow cone on its head?" asked Shaggy.

"No, we're going to lure it onto a water ride and then leave it high and dry," Velma said.

"And the highest place around is the top of the Flume Plume," Daphne said.

Shaggy and Scooby shook their heads.

"Ruh-ruh," Scooby said.

"There's absolutely no way you're going

to get Scooby and me to lure that goblin onto the Flume Plume," Shaggy said. "There's absolutely nothing you can say or do."

"How about a Scooby Snack?" Daphne asked.

"Rexcept rhat!" Scooby barked happily.

Daphne tossed the treat to Scooby.

"Hey, what about me?" asked Shaggy.

"All right, here's something for you," Velma said. She tossed something over to Shaggy, who gobbled it up.

"Hey, that's my peanut butter, banana, and chocolate chip sand-wich!" Shaggy said. "Thanks, Velma."

"Here's the plan," Fred said. "Shaggy and Scooby will go up onto the Flume Plume. When the goblin shows up, Velma will signal Daphne.

Daphne will signal me. I'll be in the pump house and use the tool to shut off the water."

"But how will Scooby and I get away from El Goblino?" asked Shaggy.

"With this," Fred said, holding up Ziggy Bones's skateboard. "Tippy Torrance took it away from Ziggy, remember?"

"We'll use Ziggy's idea. You two can skateboard down the dry slide," Velma said. "There'll be more than enough water at the bottom for a safe splash landing." She handed the skateboard to Shaggy.

"Now let's get going," Fred said.

The gang walked back to the Flume Plume to get into position. Shaggy and Scooby followed the winding path through the fake forest and up to the top of the ride again. This time, there wasn't anyone there to operate the ride.

"Okay, Scooby," Shaggy shouted over the roar of the waterfall. "You get into the log. I'll start the ride and then jump in behind you. Got it?"

"Rot rit!" Scooby yelled back. He took the skateboard from Shaggy and climbed into the giant log. "Ready!"

Just as Shaggy was about to push the button, he felt a tap on his shoulder. He turned around and came face-to-face with the goblin!

"Zoinks!" Shaggy cried and jumped into the log too.

The goblin pushed the START button and jumped into the log behind them.

"Scooby-Doo!" Shaggy yelled. "Behind you!"

Scooby slowly turned around and saw the blue goblin sitting behind him.

"Beautiful view from up here, don't you think?" the goblin asked.

"Rikes!" Scooby whimpered.

As the log followed the twisting path, the goblin's evil laugh filled Scooby's ears. Just as

51

the log reached the edge of the big drop, it stopped. All of the water stopped, too.

"What's going on here?" the goblin shouted. Its voice echoed loudly.

"Now, Scooby!" Velma and Daphne called from below.

Scooby swallowed hard and stood up.

"Rood-rye," he said. He climbed out of the log, put the skateboard down, and gave himself the tiniest little push. The goblin realized what was happening and sprang into action. As Scooby disappeared over the edge, the goblin grabbed onto his tail.

Scooby skateboarded down the steep slide with the goblin bouncing along behind him.

"Whoooooooaaaaaaahhhhhh!"

The goblin crashed into an enormous pile of inner tubes stacked up next to the ride.

Chapter 9

Velma helped Scooby out of the water. "Are you all right, Scooby?" she asked.

Scooby shook the water off his body, soaking her.

"Reah, Ri'm all right," he said.

Fred and Daphne ran over to find the goblin stuck inside three inner tubes. Tippy Torrance also came over.

"You're just in time, Ms. Torrance," Fred said. "Would you like to see who's really behind all this?"

"You bet," Tippy answered. She reached

over and pulled off the goblin's mask. "Bruno Meisterhoffen!" she gasped.

"Just as we suspected," Daphne said.

"You did?" Tippy asked. "How did you know?"

"Simple detective work," Velma answered. "It all started when we found our first clue: a torn piece of a picture."

Fred showed the picture to Tippy, who immediately recognized it.

"That's my arm," she said. "This is from a picture of me."

"And when we thought about who would have a picture of you to leave behind, we immediately thought of three possible suspects," Fred said.

"Bruno Meisterhoffen, who made the picture of you in his water polo uniform," Daphne said. "Ziggy Bones, who put you on a skateboard."

"I remember those two, but who was the third?" asked Tippy.

"Me," Mr. Glumley said from behind her. "I was mad at you for firing me so I got a little carried away and did this." He showed her the picture with her teeth blacked out. "I remembered I left a few more of my tools here, so I'll just get them and leave."

"Hold on, Mr. Glumley," Tippy said. "Now that I know that Bruno was behind all this, I think I'm going to want you to stay after all."

Mr. Glumley smiled.

"Then we found the next clue by the Lazy River ride," Velma said. She showed them the special wrench. "And we knew the only people with access to that kind of a tool would be Mr. Glumley, who works here, and Bruno."

"Meisterhoffen Plumbing Supply!" said Tippy. "Of course!"

"Finally, we found this," Daphne said. She showed them the red-white-and-blue rubbery thing.

"A swim cap," Tippy said. "The same design as the water polo uniform."

"Exactly," Fred said. "Once we found this,

we knew that only Mr. Meisterhoffen would have something like it."

"But why would you do this, Bruno?" asked Tippy. "Is this all because I wouldn't be part of your water polo dream?"

Bruno gnashed his teeth and then spoke. "Don't flatter yourself, Torrance," he said angrily. "You have something much more valuable that I wanted."

Tippy looked puzzled.

"Water," Bruno said. "The town rejected my plans because they were concerned with the amount of water my water polo stadium would need. I planned to shut down Ocean Land so I could have access to all of this wonderful water. And I would have gotten away with it, too, if it weren't for those kids and their water-loving, skateboarding mutt!"

"Heard enough, Ms. Torrance?" asked Daphne.

"Speaking of hearing enough, how did

Bruno get his voice all over the park?" Tippy asked.

"With this," Velma said. She took a small microphone out of the goblin's mask. "Mr. Meisterhoffen simply used a wireless microphone that he tuned to the frequency of the park's PA system."

"You kids are absolutely amazing," Tippy said. "You solved the mystery, saved Ocean Land, and even helped Mr. Glumley get his

job back. Is there anything I can do to thank you?"

"Ro cone?" Scooby asked.

"Scooby, you can have as many snow cones as you want," Tippy said. "But I've got an even better idea. Starting tomorrow, Ocean Land will offer its guests a brand-new ride that combines the fun of water and the thrill of skateboarding. And we'll call it the 'Scooby Plume'!"

Everyone laughed as Scooby grabbed the microphone from Velma. His "Rooby-Rooby-roo!" echoed throughout the park.